The Happy Prince

PICTURE WINDOW BOOKS
a capstone imprint

First published in the United States in 2011
by Picture Window Books
A Capstone Imprint
151 Good Counsel Drive
P.O. Box 669
Mankato, Minnesota 56002
www.capstonepub.com

© 2008, Edizioni El S.r.l., Trieste Italy in IL PRINCIPE FELICE

Library of Congress Cataloging-in-Publication Data is available on the Library of Congress website.
ISBN 978-1-4048-6500-6 (library binding)

Summary: A swallow and a statue help those in need in this retelling of Oscar Wilde's classic story.

Art Director: Kay Fraser
Graphic Designer: Emily Harris
Production Specialist: Michelle Biedscheid

Printed in the United States of America in North Mankato, Minnesota.
092010

005933CGS11

The Happy Prince

Retold by Roberto Piumini

Illustrated by Alessandra Cimatoribus

Once upon a time, there was a statue of a prince who had died. During his life, the young man had known only joy, so he was known as the Happy Prince.

The statue stood in the center of a city, shining in the sunlight. A layer of gold leaves covered his body. His eyes were two sapphires, and atop his sword was a glowing red ruby.

One autumn day, a swallow landed at the statue's feet to rest. Suddenly, a drop of water fell on the bird. It was a tear from the statue. "Why are you crying?" asked the swallow.

"When I was alive, I never left my palace, so I knew nothing of sorrow," answered the prince. "But from here I can see so much sadness, it makes me cry."

The statue continued. "Over there, in that house, I can see a woman sewing. Her little boy is sick with a fever. He is asking for oranges, and she has nothing but water. Please, will you bring her the ruby from my sword so she can buy him some oranges?"

"Winter is coming. I must leave now for the warm land of Egypt," said the swallow.

"Help me just this once," pleaded the prince.

So the swallow picked out the great ruby and carried it across the city to the poor woman's house. Entering through a hole in the roof, he laid the ruby on the table. Hearing the soft noise, the woman lifted her head from her sewing. She could not believe her eyes.

It was too late to leave for Egypt, so the tired bird returned to the statue and fell asleep.

When he awoke the next morning, the sun was already high overhead. The sky was filled with the last birds heading for warmer lands.

The swallow flew around a bit to warm his wings. Then he announced, "I'm going to Egypt! I'll fly over land and sea, and in a week I'll sleep on the warm stones of the pyramids!"

The prince said, "I see a young man in a small attic across the city. He is trying to finish a play, but he is too cold to write. Before you go, take one of my sapphire eyes to him, so he can buy some firewood."

"I cannot take one of your eyes!" exclaimed the swallow.

"Don't worry. I won't feel a thing," said the prince.

So the swallow plucked out the gem and flew to the small attic. He entered through the window and set the sapphire on the table. The young writer was speechless with surprise.

The swallow returned to the statue, where he again fell asleep at the prince's feet. The days were now short, and the evenings grew colder. The prince tried to soak up the sun's warmth and give it to the sleeping swallow.

The next morning when the bird awoke, he looked up at the empty sky. The sun was shining, but it was cold. Winter had arrived.

The swallow declared, "I am off to Egypt, prince! I'll take your greetings to the pyramids and the Nile. It is too bad you never left your palace when you were alive! But I promise, when I return in the spring, I'll tell you all about everything I saw there."

The prince listened in silence. Then with his quiet voice, he said, "Look down, my friend."

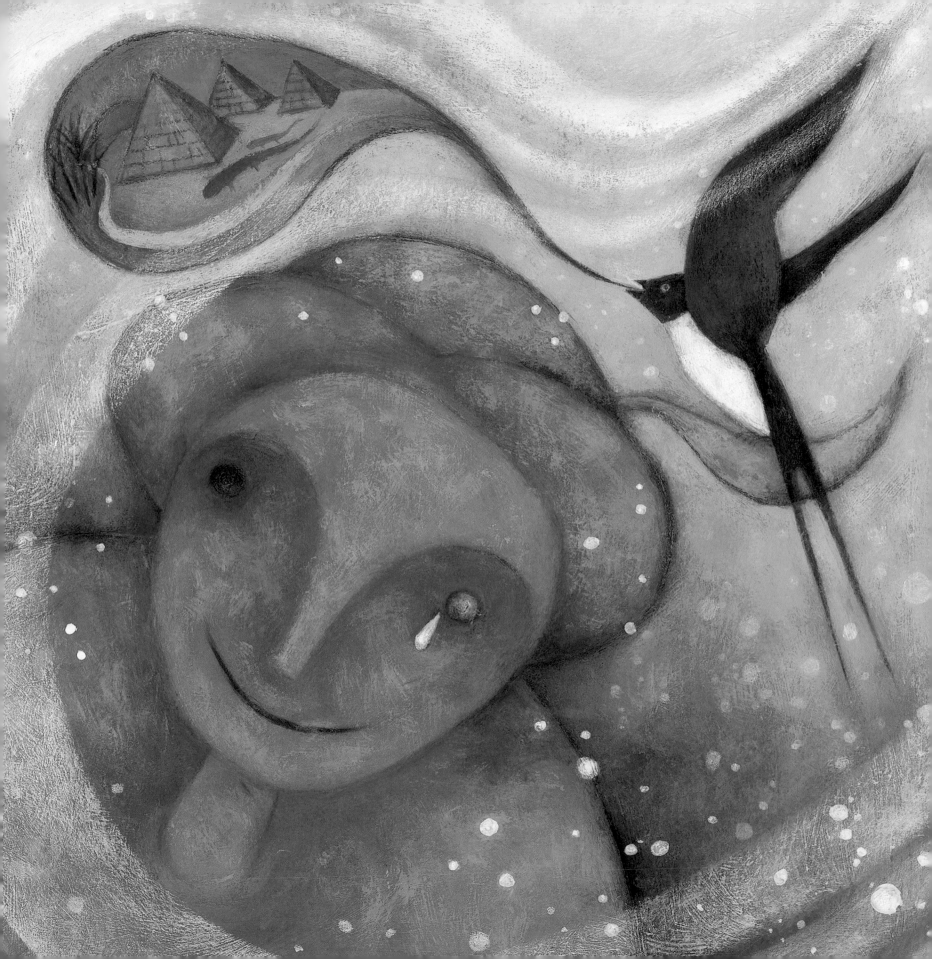

The bird looked down into the square below the statue and saw a little match girl. She was very pale and thin.

"That match girl has let her matches fall in the gutter, and they are all spoiled," said the prince. "Her father will certainly be angry when she goes home."

"You don't want to give her your remaining eye, do you?" asked the swallow.

The prince didn't answer, but his silence spoke for him. It was exactly what he wanted. The swallow plucked out the prince's other eye. He dove down with it and slipped it into the little girl's hand. She looked at the jewel happily and ran off.

A cold wind ruffled the swallow's feathers. "Now you must fly away to Egypt, my friend," said the prince. "I thank you for all you've done. Even though I cannot see, when you return you can tell me about your adventures. Then I'll be able to picture everything in my mind!"

"I cannot leave you now, alone and blind," said the bird. "I'll stay with you always."

The prince could not change the swallow's mind, so the statue did what he could to make the bird more comfortable. He tried to soak up sun during the day and spread it to his feet at night so that the little bird could be warmed.

During these winter days, the prince often asked the bird to fly over the city. He said, "Then come back and tell me what you have seen."

When the swallow flew around the city, he always returned to the prince with stories of people who did not have food or shelter.

"Take them my leaves of gold," said the prince. So the swallow picked them off, one by one, and took them to the poor.

It got even colder, and the swallow was the only bird left in the city. The winter was hard on the little bird, and he grew weaker with each day.

After the swallow delivered the last gold leaf to a hungry child on the other side of the city, he returned to his spot at the prince's feet. The bird knew he was going to die.

He rose in flight one last time, lightly touched the prince's cheek with his beak, then fell dead at his feet.

Feeling the kiss and the light fall of the bird, the prince realized what had happened. Tears fell from his eyes, and they froze in an instant.

The next morning, the mayor of the city noticed the statue. "How shabby the prince's statue has become! Let's melt him down. We can use the metal to make a statue of me."

The statue was melted in a furnace, but the statue's lead heart remained solid. It was thrown onto a dustheap where the dead swallow was also lying.

Now God was watching this scene from heaven. He said to one of his angels, "Bring me the two most precious things in the city."

So the angel flew down and returned with the heart and the bird. And God welcomed the two friends, saying, "This little bird and this Happy Prince will sing in my house for evermore."

✎ Fairy Tale Follow-Up ✎

1. Why do you think the prince never left his palace when he was alive?

2. What do you think the woman with the sick son thought when she saw the large ruby that the swallow brought her?

3. Why did the swallow want to go to Egypt? Did he need to go? Why or why not?

4. Do you think it was right for the prince to keep asking for the bird's help?

5. What do you think would have happened to the little match girl if she had not received the jewel?

6. At the end of the story, the Happy Prince and the swallow are called the two most precious things in the city. What made them precious?

♋ Glossary ♋

attic (AT-ik)—a space in a building just under the roof

furnace (FUR-niss)—a large enclosed metal chamber in which fuel is burned to make heat

gutter (GUHT-ur)—a low area on a roadside that carries away surface water

match girl (MACH GURL)—a girl whose job it was to sell matches to people on the street, a common job in the 1800s

Nile (NIE-el)—a long river in Africa

precious (PRESH-uhss)—very special

pyramids (PEER-uh-midz)—ancient Egyptian stone monuments where pharaohs and their treasures were buried

sapphires (SA-fi-urz)—clear, deep-blue precious stones

swallow (SWAHL-oh)—a migrating bird with long wings and a forked tail

Fun Facts about Swallows

The title of this story may be *The Happy Prince*, but without the swallow, the prince wouldn't have been able to help anyone. Swallows may be small birds, but they make a big impact. Did you know . . .

Swallows live in a variety of habitats. Farmland, cities, highways, marshes, lakeshores, barns, bridges, and culverts can all be homes to swallows.

The name "swallow" comes from the way the birds catch insects while flying, eating them up with a swallow.

Swallows have been known to take a bath without even stopping their flight. While flying over a pond, they swoop down, take a dip in the water, then swoop back up without ever resting.

Farmers usually like swallows because they feast mainly on pesky bugs like grasshoppers and crickets. Tree swallows also eat berries and seeds.

Female barn swallows are most attracted to males with dark reddish chests and longer tails.

Swallows often mate for life.

Swallows build cup-shaped nests out of mud. Then they line them with feathers and grass.

Both the male and female swallows build a nest together. While they are building, the couple can take up to a thousand trips to get mud.

Swallows can feed their young while flying.

Swallows fly in groups. They journey about 600 miles per day.

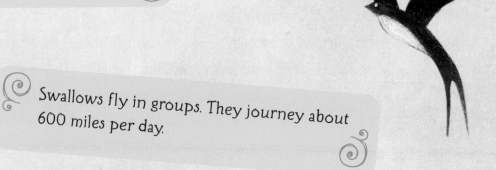

About the Author

Roberto Piumini lives and works in his native Italy. He has worked with children as both a teacher and a theater actor/entertainer. He credits these experiences for inspiring the youthful language of his many books. With his crisp and imaginative way of dealing with every kind of subject, Roberto charms his young readers. His award-winning books, for both children and adults, have been translated into many languages.

About the Illustrator

Alessandra Cimatoribus was born in Spilimbergo in Friuli, Italy, in 1967. She continues to live and work in Spilimbergo. She attended the International School of Graphics in Venice. Her work includes illustrations for children's books, games, packaging, advertising, and designs for theater costumes.